Pug's New Puppy

Read all the Diary of a Pug books!

DIARY OF A PUG
Pug Blasts Off
1
DIARY OF A PUG
Pug's Snow Day
2
DIARY OF A PUG
Paws for a Cause
3
DIARY OF A PUG
Pug's Got Talent
4
DIARY OF A PUG
Scaredy-Pug
5
DIARY OF A PUG
Pug's Sleepover
6
DIARY OF A PUG
Pug's Road Trip
7
DIARY OF A PUG
Pug's New Puppy
8
DIARY OF A PUG
Pug the Prince
9

More books coming soon!

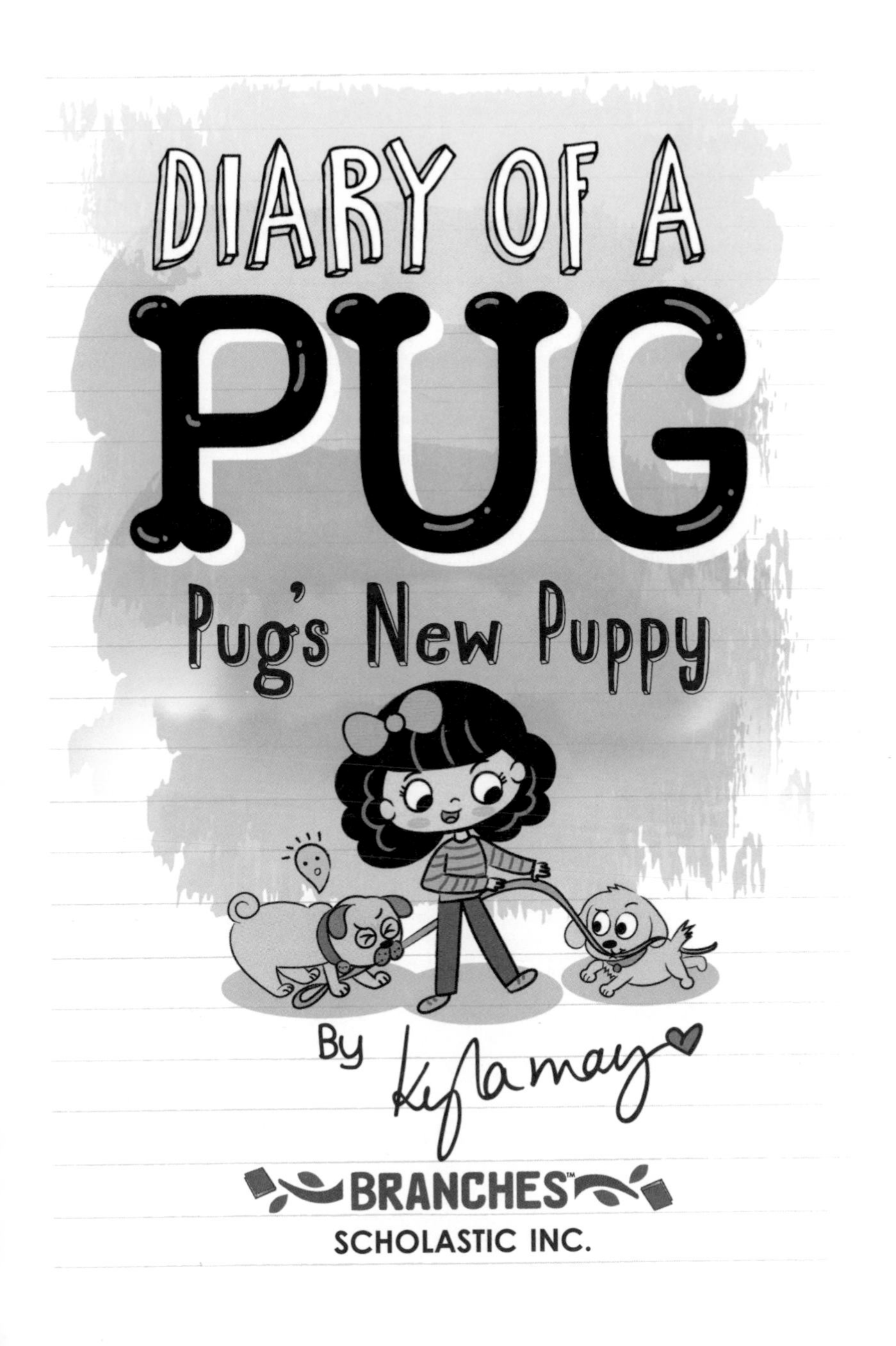
DIARY OF A
PUG
Pug's New Puppy
By Kyla May
BRANCHES™
SCHOLASTIC INC.

I dedicate this book to my new puppy love, Harlow, my golden retriever.

Special thanks to Madelyn Rosenberg

Library of Congress Cataloging-in-Publication Data

Names: May, Kyla, author, illustrator. Title: Pug's new puppy / by Kyla May. Description: First edition. | New York : Branches/Scholastic Inc., 2023. | Series: Diary of a pug; #8 | Audience: Ages 6-8 | Audience: Grades 2-3 | Summary: Bub the pug and his human, Bella, cannot wait to teach Nana's new pup, Harlow, some new tricks, but they soon realize training a puppy is not as easy as they thought. Identifiers: LCCN 2022006853 (print) | ISBN 9781338713534 (paperback) | ISBN 9781338713541 (library binding) Subjects: CYAC: Pug—Fiction. | Dogs—Fiction. | Dogs—Training—Fiction. | Animals—Infancy—Fiction. | Human-animal relationships—Fiction. | Diaries—Fiction. | Humorous stories. | BISAC: JUVENILE FICTION/ Readers / Chapter Books | JUVENILE FICTION / Animals / Dogs | LCGFT: Animal fiction. | Humorous fiction. Classification: LCC PZ7.M4535 Pwe 2023 (print) | DDC [Fic]—dc23 LC record available at https://lccn.loc.gov/2022006853

978-1-338-71353-4 (paperback) / 978-1-338-71354-1 (reinforced library binding)

10 9 8 7 6 5 4 3 2 1 23 24 25 26 27

Printed in China 62
First edition, October 2023
Edited by Mia Licciardi
Book design by Kyla May and Christian Zelaya

Table of Contents

Chapter 1

PUP-ULATION EXPLOSION

FRIDAY

Dear Diary,

It's me, **BUB**. You'll never guess who's coming to stay with us!

But before I fill you in, here are some things to know about me.

I'm great at sniffing out style!

I make many different faces:

Worried Face
I Love Treats Face
TREATS
Sorry I Ate All the Treats Face
TREATS

Here are some of my favorite things:
PEANUT BUTTER
BEAR
BELLA

Here are some things that get on my nerves:

DUCHESS

Other people live here, too!
Did someone say something?

NUTZ

Hand it over, Nutz.
It's mine! It says "Nuts" right on the jar!
NUTS

And **WATER**!

That includes baths, even though that's how I got my full name, BARON VON BUBBLES. When Bella first brought me home, she had a tub of fluffy bubbles waiting. Who knew water was hiding under them?

Back to our houseguest. Today, just before dinner, the phone rang. It was Bella's Nana!

What? When?
This should be interesting.
Shhh! I'm listening!

A new puppy!
You can count on us!
You can count on SOME of us.

When Bella hung up, she shared the big news.

Guess what? We're getting a puppy!

It's just for a week, while Nana goes to visit her sister.

I can show the new kid a thing or two!

But taking care of a small puppy is a BIG responsibility. I got a little nervous. You know what I do when I'm nervous. I get a little gassy.

Don't worry, Bubby! We've got this!
I hope so!
!!!

Bella thinks we can handle it. We'll find out tomorrow!

Chapter 2

IT'S TIME TO GET PUP

SATURDAY

Dear Diary,

By the time Nana brought the puppy over, I was ready.

Welcome, Harlow. Look, Bella bought us matching sweaters!
Her name is Harlow.
She's so cute!
Arf!

I put together a welcoming committee. It was Duchess, plus Luna, my best friend. (She and her human, Jack, live next door.)

Oh, good. Another minion.
Puppy!
Nutz? What are you doing here?!
Awesome! A new source for treats!
Arf!

Harlow ran around the yard. She was fast!

Harlow! Come!

By the time Bella caught her, we were all out of breath.

I've been trying to teach her to sit and stay. When I get back, she's going to puppy school. I love her. But she's impossible.
Im-paw-ssible, you mean.
Don't worry, Nana. We'll take good care of her.

After Nana left, I showed the puppy the finer things in life. I was sure we would have lots in common.

And this is peanut butter!
Arf?

But what Harlow really liked was Duchess's cat food.

Harlow has good taste. But keep her away from my dinner!
Arf!
CAT FOOD

And get this—she wouldn't even try on her new sweater. She just ran!

How does Nana do this alone?
Now I know why Nana wants to send Harlow to puppy school.
I know! We can train Harlow ourselves! Nana will be so surprised!
If it works!

Bella decided we would open a Puppy School!

We'll show Harlow how to walk on a leash!
And rock a sweater!
We'll show her how to stay away from my dinner!
CAT FOOD

We need a plan.
We should also teach Harlow how to fetch, sit, and roll over. And how to high-five!
I'll high-five to that!

Jack and I will be teachers.
And I have special roles for you and Luna, Bubby. You will be our assistants!

An assistant? Meaning I just help the teacher? Hmph. I could BE the teacher, Diary. No one knows more about being a dog than me! This will be easy . . . right?

Chapter 3

ALL TIED PUP

SUNDAY

Dear Diary,

On the first day of Puppy School, Harlow woke up early.

What time is it?
Her nickname should be "Rooster."
I need my beauty rest.
zzz

Since we were up, Bella made a schedule for Puppy School.

PUPPY SCHOOL SCHEDULE
Sunday: Walk on a leash
Monday: Fetch
Tuesday: Sit
Wednesday: Roll over
Thursday: Learn to high-five
Friday: Review. Graduation!

I made a graduation cap for Harlow. She hadn't learned anything yet, but with me as her teacher, she'd be at the head of her class! And the cap was fashion at its finest!

Today's lesson was how to walk on a leash. It didn't start well.

We decided to get some help.

What time is it?
Early. Very, very early.

Bella tried to show Harlow how to walk next to her. But puppies do not know what "next to" means.

That's not "next to," that's "around"!
That's not "next to," that's "between"!

And that's upside down!

Jack tried next.

Come on, Harlow. Let's go!
Yip!

It didn't end well.

After a few more tries, Jack and Luna had to head home.

What a tiring morning! I need a nap. Can you watch Harlow, Bubby?
This is my chance to be the teacher!

We went outside so Bella could sleep. I started teaching! First, I explained the history of fashion.

They called it the poodle skirt!
Your fashion class isn't very paw-pular.

Next, I showed Harlow how to make my famous faces.

This is the Sorry I Woke You Up Early Face.
Arf!

Harlow wasn't sorry.

This is the Sitting Still Face. Watch Bear! Bear is great at sitting still.

All Harlow wanted to do was run.

She ran and looked at trees.
She ran and chased butterflies.
She even chased a bee!
Harlow! Stop! Danger!
Buzz off.

I was glad when Bella came back outside. She always knows what to do.

Still on the run, Harlow? Maybe we can tire you out.
That's mission im-paw-ssible.
Arf arf arf arf arf!

Will Harlow be calmer tomorrow, Diary? I hope so . . .

Chapter 4

LET'S WASH PUP

MONDAY

Dear Diary,

Harlow woke up early again. She didn't bark. That's because she found something to do. I mean, something to chew!

?

The puppy ate my homework!
That's the oldest excuse in the world.
And the truest!
BELLA
SOLAR SYSTEM PROJECT

But Bella forgave Harlow right away.

You're still so cute! I can't stay mad at you.
Really? We've seen cuter.
You mean me, right, Bubby-kins?

Today's lesson is fetching. But we can't have Puppy School until after Human School. Keep Harlow out of trouble!
We'll teach her something, too!

We could start the fetching lessons now. Why wait?
My thoughts exactly. I'm a fetching expert!

Luna threw a ball.

I threw a stick.

Nutz threw an acorn.

Did we ask for your help?
You need all the help you can get.

He was right, of course. Harlow did not fetch anything.

All she wanted to fetch was a butterfly. She chased it around the tree . . .

Through the flower bed . . .

And into Luna's yard.

SPLASH!
Uh-oh!

Harlow had jumped right into Luna's pool!

I'd better fly!
Look! She wants to learn to swim!

But Harlow didn't swim for long, Diary. She jumped out of the pool and ran straight over to me.

She already knows how to dry off!
I didn't think they were calling for rain.
Teaching is a "ruff" job! Maybe it's a good thing I'm only an assistant.

Bella and Jack came home and gave us all snuggles.

You worked on fetching! Good thinking! Show us what you learned, Harlow.

You can guess how that went, Diary. But then, Harlow did fetch something.

That's not what we asked her to get.
But it's a start!

At the end of the day, Bear showed Harlow how to get a good night's sleep.

You're a good role model, Bear!
Tomorrow is a new day, Harlow. We'll try a new skill, too. An easy one!

Tomorrow has to go better, Diary. It <u>has</u> to!

Chapter 5

PUP, PUP, AND AWAY!

TUESDAY

Dear Diary,

Today's lesson was sitting. Bella worked with Harlow before school. They didn't make any progress.

Duchess and I tried, too.

Sit like me. You'll look royal.
It's not hard, Harlow. Watch me!

Harlow didn't want to sit. All she wanted to do was CHEW.

That's not food!
I love the couch . . . but not enough to eat it.
Maybe we should go outside.
Agreed.

When we got outside, Nutz was waiting.

Welcome, student!
Nutz, you are not a part of Puppy School.
But you need me! Remember how fetch went yesterday?

Are we still fetching? Harlow, fetch Bub's peanut butter!
You wish, Nutz. Today's lesson is sitting.
Hey! Good job, Harlow!
She won't fetch the peanut butter, but I bet she'd fetch the couch!

At the word "couch," Harlow ran inside.

But when she came back out, she was not carrying the couch. She was carrying Bear!

How dare she, Diary? Bear is so VERY important to me.

Harlow! Come back!
This calls for an expert.
And who would that be?
Me!

Nutz is fast. And sneaky. It turns out we did need him!

Harlow ran into Jack and Luna's yard. She stopped to watch a bird. Snatch! Nutz grabbed Bear and passed Bear to me.

Thank you, thank you, thank you!
You can thank me with some peanut butter.
Um, is Bear okay?

I looked Bear over from head to toe. Bear was NOT okay. Bear's ear was hurt!

Hang on, Bear!
Bella will know what to do!
Arf?

Chapter 6

Chapter 6

PUPS AND DOWNS

WEDNESDAY

Dear Diary,

Yesterday afternoon, Harlow watched me pace outside.

Look what you did to Bear!
Bear will be purr-fectly fine. Bella will help when she gets home!
?

Finally, Human School was over for the day.

What is it, Bubby?
What's going on?
Bear is hurt!

We rushed Bear inside.

I wonder what happened.
We don't have to wonder. But Harlow IS just a puppy.
This will require surgery.
Oh no. I'm going to faint.
Shhh. It will be okay.
Don't you mean "fart"?
But would it?

Diary, you will be happy to know that Dr. Bella saved Bear!

I can't look!

This morning, I gave Nutz a big jar of thank-you peanut butter.

Thanks for saving Bear yesterday!

Then Nutz and Duchess helped out with Puppy School. Bella's schedule said today's lesson was "rolling over."

Roll over, Harlow.

I knew I should help, but I was still upset about Bear.

The more Harlow learns, the easier it will be to keep her safe.
But who will keep Bear safe?
?

Just then, Harlow dropped a dandelion in front of me.

Look! She's learning to fetch.
She's saying she's sorry.

But I wasn't ready to forgive her. I showed Harlow my Go Away Face.

Hmmm . . . I think Puppy School needs a recess.
A LONG recess.
Sounds great to me.

Recess was great. I took a nap in the sun. So did Luna.

zzz

It was quiet. (Except for Luna's snoring.)

A little too quiet.

Where's Harlow?
?

I checked all over the yard.
And Luna's yard.
Has anyone seen Harlow?
Not me.
?
Have you seen Harlow?
?
Not since the start of recess.

I was worried, Diary. What if Harlow thought my Go Away Face meant I wanted her to go away FOREVER?

Bubby, what's wrong now?
Harlow's gone! And it's all my fault!

We searched for Harlow all afternoon.

Bella made a poster so everyone would know Harlow was missing.

?
BUB PHOTOS

Meanwhile, I checked the storage closet. No Harlow. But I found something else: my puppy pictures!

Harlow reminds me of you when you were little.
I was cute! But it looks like I wasn't perfect.

Maybe I had been too hard on Harlow. When I was a puppy, I made mistakes, too. I HAD to find Harlow. I needed to apologize.

Chapter 7

PUPPY PANIC

THURSDAY

Dear Diary,

This morning, Bella and Jack stayed home from school. We split up and searched again. I noticed something in the kitchen: muddy paw prints.

Muddy paw prints.
And a muddy line?
Those weren't here last night . . .

I followed the mud tracks through the house and down the hall.

Bella

And there, right in the middle of Bella's bed was . . .

. . . something in a red cap? It was that garden statue Harlow had brought Bella during fetch.

I saw muddy paw prints leading to the closet. I followed those, too.

?

I found Harlow, Diary! But she wouldn't come out.

HARLOW?

I knew what I had to say.

I'm sorry, Harlow.
I know you didn't mean to hurt Bear.
You're just a puppy. You're still learning.
Will you come out now?
We've missed you.

Nothing happened for a moment. Then Harlow stood up. She gave me the I'm Sorry Face. (At least I'd taught her one thing!) She wagged her tail!

A minute later, everyone else rushed into the room.

You found her, Bub!
Good work, Bubby-kins.
Arf!

Still working on how to fetch, huh, Harlow?

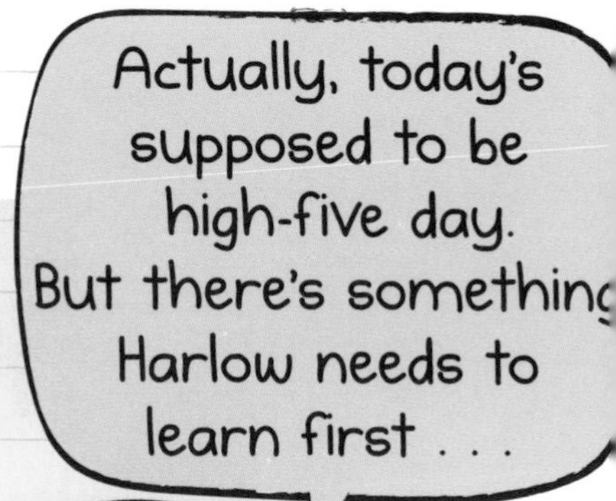
Actually, today's supposed to be high-five day. But there's something Harlow needs to learn first . . .

How to take a bath!

Harlow liked the bath. I didn't. But we did find something we both loved: snuggles!

We didn't teach Harlow everything on our list, but Nana will still be proud. She comes home tomorrow.
Z Z Z

Will Harlow wear her graduation cap tomorrow? Or eat it?

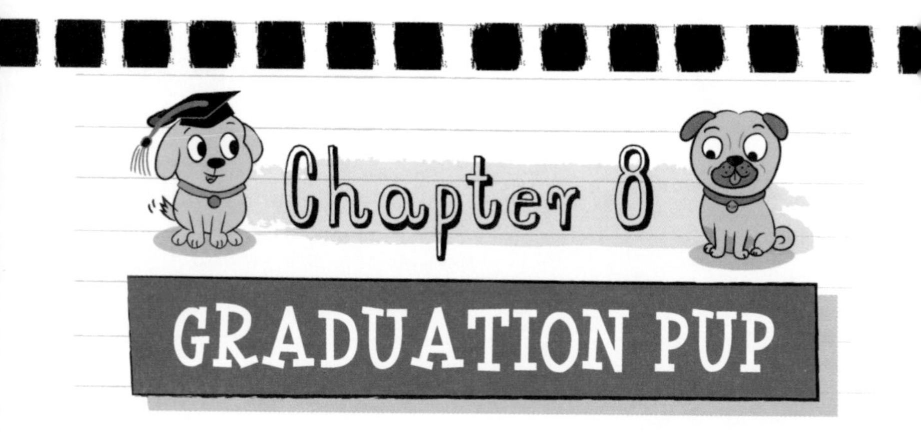

Chapter 8

GRADUATION PUP

FRIDAY

Dear Diary,

I spent a happy morning outside with Harlow. It turns out chasing butterflies is fun!

Luna splashed with Harlow in the pool.

And Duchess let Harlow eat some of her cat food!

I like to encourage her taste for fine dining.
I'm gonna miss this kid.
CAT FOOD

I was going to miss Harlow, too. I was the teacher, but she taught <u>me</u> a lot! Mostly, she taught me that I still have more to learn . . . even if I am the World's Cutest Pug.

When Bella and Jack got home from school, we got everything ready for graduation. Then, we waited for Nana.

HAPPY GRADUATION!!

She finally arrived. Bella's mom came, too.

What's all this?
Puppy School!

We took Nana and Bella's mom to Luna's yard to show them how Harlow liked to splash . . . and shake.

How clever! She can shake herself dry!
Watch out!

Bella asked Harlow to sit and roll over. She didn't do it in the right order. But that was okay.

Sit, Harlow!

Then Bella threw a ball for Harlow to fetch. She brought back something else.

Not quite a ball, but a great skill!

Harlow showed Nana her new faces.
Cat Food Face
I Want to Chew on the Couch Face
We got in one last snuggle before it was time for them to leave.
She's learned so much!
Keep an eye on your couch.

And guess what? Harlow wore her graduation cap!

She'll eat it before they get to Nana's.
It might taste good with peanut butter.
We'll miss you, Harlow! Come back soon!

About the Creator

Kyla May

Kyla May is an Australian illustrator, writer, and designer. Before creating children's books, Kyla created animation and designed toys. She lives by the beach in Victoria, Australia, with her three daughters, two cats, and three dogs, including her golden retriever puppy called Harlow. The character of Bub was inspired by her daughter's pug called Bear.

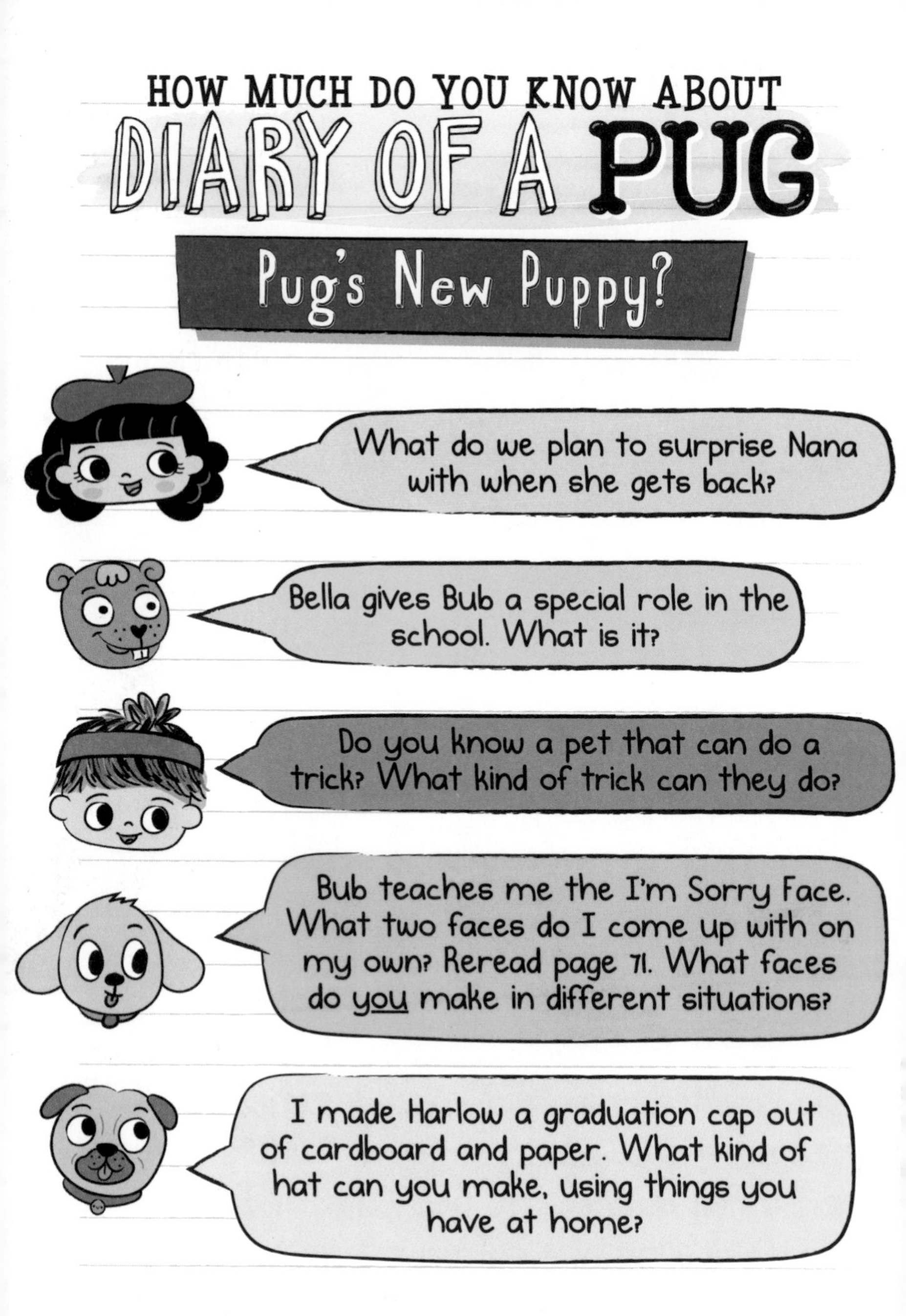
HOW MUCH DO YOU KNOW ABOUT
DIARY OF A PUG
Pug's New Puppy?
What do we plan to surprise Nana with when she gets back?
Bella gives Bub a special role in the school. What is it?
Do you know a pet that can do a trick? What kind of trick can they do?
Bub teaches me the I'm Sorry Face. What two faces do I come up with on my own? Reread page 71. What faces do you make in different situations?
I made Harlow a graduation cap out of cardboard and paper. What kind of hat can you make, using things you have at home?

scholastic.com/branches